HOUSE OF INCEST

ANAÏS NIN

HOUSE
OF
INCEST

PHOTOMONTAGES
by VAL TELBERG

THE **SWALLOW PRESS** INC.
CHICAGO

Published by
The Swallow Press Incorporated
1139 South Wabash Avenue
Chicago, Illinois 60605

This book is printed on 100% recycled paper.

ISBN 0-8040-0148-0
LIBRARY OF CONGRESS CATALOG CARD NUMBER 61-65487

ALL THAT I KNOW IS CONTAINED
IN THIS BOOK WRITTEN WITHOUT
WITNESS, AN EDIFICE WITHOUT
DIMENSION, A CITY HANGING IN
THE SKY.

The morning I got up to begin this book I coughed. Something was coming out of my throat: it was strangling me. I broke the thread which held it and yanked it out. I went back to bed and said: I have just spat out my heart.

There is an instrument called the quena made of human bones. It owes its origin to the worship of an Indian for his mistress. When she died he made a flute out of her bones. The quena has a more penetrating, more haunting sound than the ordinary flute.

Those who write know the process. I thought of it as I was spitting out my heart.

Only I do not wait for my love to die.

MY first vision of earth was water veiled. I am of the race of men and women who see all things through this curtain of sea, and my eyes are the color of water.

I looked with chameleon eyes upon the changing face of the world, looked with anonymous vision upon my uncompleted self.

I remember my first birth in water. All round me a sulphurous transparency and my bones move as if made of rubber. I sway and float, stand on boneless toes listening for distant sounds, sounds beyond the reach of human ears, see things beyond the reach of human eyes. Born full of memories of the bells of the Atlantide. Always listening for lost sounds and searching for lost colors, standing forever on the threshold like one troubled with memories, and walking with a swimming stride. I cut the air with wide-slicing fins, and swim through wall-less rooms.

Ejected from a paradise of soundlessness, cathedrals wavering at the passage of a body, like soundless music.

This Atlantide could be found again only at night, by the route of the dream. As soon as sleep covered the rigid new city, the rigidity of the new world, the heaviest portals slid open on smooth-oiled gongs and one entered the voicelessness of the dream. The terror and joy of murders accomplished in silence, in the silence of slidings and brushings. The blanket of water lying over all things stifling the voice. Only a monster brought me up on the surface by accident.

Lost in the colors of the Atlantide, the colors running into one another without frontiers. Fishes made of velvet, of organdie with lace fangs, made of spangled taffeta, of silks and feathers and whiskers, with lacquered flanks and rock crystal eyes, fishes of withered leather with gooseberry eyes, eyes like the white of egg. Flowers palpitating on stalks like sea-hearts. None of them feeling their own weight, the sea-horse moving like a feather . . .

It was like yawning. I loved the ease and the blindness and the suave voyages on the water bearing one through obstacles. The water was there to bear one like a giant bosom; there was always the water to rest on, and the water transmitted the lives and the loves, the words and the thoughts.

Far beneath the level of storms I slept. I moved within color and music as inside a sea-diamond. There were no currents of thoughts, only the caress of flow and desire mingling, touching, travelling, withdrawing, wandering — the endless bottoms of peace.

I do not remember being cold there, nor warm. No pain of cold and heat. The temperature of sleep, feverless and chilless. I do not remember being hungry. Food seeped through invisible pores. I do not remember weeping.

I felt only the caress of moving —moving into the body of another— absorbed and lost within the flesh of another, lulled by the rhythm of water, the slow palpitation of the senses, the movement of silk.

Loving without knowingness, moving without effort, in the soft current of water and desire, breathing in an ecstasy of dissolution.

I awoke at dawn, thrown up on a rock, the skeleton of a ship choked in its own sails.

THE night surrounded me, a photograph unglued from its frame. The lining of a coat ripped open like the two shells of an oyster. The day and night unglued, and I falling in between not knowing on which layer I was resting, whether it was the cold grey upper leaf of dawn, or the dark layer of night.

Sabina's face was suspended in the darkness of the garden. From the eyes a simoun wind shrivelled the leaves and turned the earth over; all things which had run a vertical course now turned in circles, round the face, around HER face. She stared with such an ancient stare, heavy luxuriant centuries flickering in deep processions. From her nacreous skin perfumes spiralled like incense. Every gesture she made quickened the rhythm of the blood and aroused a beat chant like the beat of the heart of the

desert, a chant which was the sound of her feet treading down into the blood the imprint of her face.

A voice that had traversed the centuries, so heavy it broke what it touched, so heavy I feared it would ring in me with eternal resonance; a voice rusty with the sound of curses and the hoarse cries that issue from the delta in the last paroxysm of orgasm.

Her black cape hung like black hair from her shoulders, half-draped, half-floating around her body. The web of her dress moving always a moment before she moved, as if aware of her impulses, and stirring long after she was still, like waves ebbing back to the sea. Her sleeves dropped like a sigh and the hem of her dress danced round her feet.

The steel necklace on her throat flashed like summer lightning and the sound of the steel was like the clashing of swords . . . Le pas d'acier . . . The steel of New York's skeleton buried in granite, buried standing up. Le pas d'acier . . . notes hammered on the steel-stringed guitars of the gypsies, on the steel arms of chairs dulled with her breath; steel mail curtains falling like the flail of hail, steel bars and steel barrage cracking. Her necklace thrown around the world's neck, unmeltable. She carried it like a trophy wrung of groaning machinery, to match the inhuman rhythm of her march.

The leaf fall of her words, the stained glass hues of her moods, the rust in her voice, the smoke in her mouth, her breath on my vision like human breath blinding a mirror.

Talk—half-talk, phrases that had no need to be finished, abstractions, Chinese bells played on with cotton-tipped sticks, mock orange blossoms painted on porcelain. The muffled, close, half-talk of soft-fleshed women. The men she had embraced, and the women, all washing against the resonance of my memory. Sound within sound, scene within scene, woman within woman—like acid revealing an invisible script. One woman within another eternally, in a far-reaching procession, shattering my mind into fragments, into quarter tones which no orchestral baton can ever make whole again.

The luminous mask of her face, waxy, immobile, with eyes like sentinels. Watching my sybaritic walk, and I the sibilance of her tongue. Deep into each other we turned our harlot eyes. She was an idol in Byzance, an idol dancing with legs parted; and I wrote with pollen and honey. The soft secret yielding of woman I carved into men's brains with copper words; her image I tattooed in their eyes. They were consumed by the fever of their entrails, the indissoluble poison of legends. If the torrent failed to engulf them, or did they extricate themselves, I haunted their memory with the tale they wished to forget. All that was swift and malevolent in woman might be ruthlessly destroyed, but who would destroy the illusion on which I laid her to sleep each night? We lived in Byzance. Sabina and I, until our hearts bled from the precious stones on our foreheads, our bodies tired of the weight of brocades, our nostrils burned with the smoke of perfumes; and when we had passed into other centuries they enclosed us in copper frames. Men recognized her always: the same effulgent face, the same rust voice. And she and I, we recognized each other; I her face and she my legend.

Around my pulse she put a flat steel bracelet and my pulse beat as she willed, losing its human cadence, thumping like a savage in orgiastic frenzy. The lamentations of flutes, the double chant of wind through our slender bones, the cracking of our bones distantly remembered when on beds of down the worship we inspired turned to lust.

As we walked along, rockets burst from the street lamps; we swallowed the asphalt road with a jungle roar and the houses with their closed eyes and geranium eyelashes; swallowed the telegraph poles trembling with messages; swallowed stray cats, trees, hills, hedges, Sabina's labyrinthian smile on the keyhole. The door moaning, opening. Her smile closed. A nightingale disleafing melliferous honeysuckle. Honey-suckled. Fluted fingers. The house opened its green gate mouth and swallowed us. The bed was floating.

The record was scratched, the crooning broken. The pieces cut our feet. It was dawn and she was lost. I put back the houses on the road, aligned the telegraph poles along the river and the stray cats jumping across the road. I put back the hills. The road came out of my mouth like a velvet ribbon—it lay there serpentine. The houses opened their eyes. The keyhole had an ironic curve, like a question mark. The woman's mouth.

I was carrying her fetiches, her marionettes, her fortune teller's cards worn at the corners like the edge of a wave. The windows of the city were stained and splintered with rainlight and the blood she drew from me with each lie, each deception. Beneath the skin of her cheeks I saw ashes: would she die before we had joined in perfidious union? The eyes, the hands, the senses that only women have.

There is no mockery between women. One lies down at peace as on one's own breast.

Sabina was no longer embracing men and women. Within the fever of her restlessness the world was losing its human shape. She was losing the human power to fit body to body in human completeness. She was delimiting the horizons, sinking into planets without axis, losing her polarity and the divine knowledge of integration, of fusion. She was spreading herself like the night over the universe and found no god to lie with. The other half belonged to the sun, and she was at war with the sun and light. She would tolerate no bars of light on open books, no orchestration of ideas knitted by a single theme; she would not be covered by the sun, and half the universe belonged to him; she was turning her serpent back to that alone which might overshadow her own stature giving her the joy of fecundation.

Come away with me, Sabina, come to my island. Come to my island of red peppers sizzling over slow braseros, Moorish earthen jars catching the gold water, palm trees, wild cats fighting, at dawn a donkey sobbing, feet on coral reefs and sea-anemones, the body covered with long seaweeds, Melisande's hair hanging over the balcony at the Opera Comique, inexorable diamond sunlight, heavy nerveless hours in the violaceous shadows, ash-colored rocks and olive trees, lemon trees with lemons hung like lanterns at a garden party, bamboo shoots forever trembling, soft-sounding espadrilles, pomegranate spurting blood, a flute-like Moorish chant, long and insistent, of the ploughmen, trilling, swearing, trilling and cursing, dropping perspiration on the earth with the seeds.

Your beauty drowns me, drowns the core of me. When your beauty burns me I dissolve as

I never dissolved before man. From all men I was different, and myself, but I see in you that part of me which is you. I feel you in me; I feel my own voice becoming heavier, as if I were drinking you in, every delicate thread of resemblance being soldered by fire and one no longer detects the fissure.

Your lies are not lies, Sabina. They are arrows flung out of your orbit by the strength of your fantasy. To nourish illusion. To destroy reality. I will help you: it is I who will invent lies for you and with them we will traverse the world. But behind our lies I am dropping Ariadne's golden thread—for the greatest of all joys is to be able to retrace one's lies, to return to the source and sleep one night a year washed of all superstructures.

Sabina, you made your impression upon the world. I passed through it like a ghost. Does anyone notice the owl in the tree at night, the bat which strikes the window pane while others are talking, the eyes which reflect like water and drink like blotting paper, the pity which flickers quietly like candlelight, the understanding on which people lay themselves to sleep?

DOES ANYONE KNOW WHO I AM?

Even my voice came from other worlds. I was embalmed in my own secret vertigoes. I was suspended over the world, seeing what road I could tread without treading down even clay or grass. My step was a sentient step; the mere crepitation of gravel could arrest my walk.

When I saw you, Sabina, I chose my body.

I will let you carry me into the fecundity of destruction. I choose a body then, a face, a voice. I become you. And you become me. Silence the sensational course of your body and you will see in me, intact, your own fears, your own pities. You will see love which was excluded from the passions given you, and I will see the passions excluded from love. Step out of your role and rest yourself on the core of your true desires. Cease for a moment your violent deviations. Relinquish the furious indomitable strain.

I will take them up.

Cease trembling and shaking and gasping and cursing and find again your core which I am. Rest from twistedness, distortion, deformations. For an hour you will be me; that is, the other half of yourself. The half you lost. What you burnt, broke, and tore is still in my hands: I am the keeper of fragile things and I have kept of you what is indissoluble.

Even the world and the sun cannot show their two faces at once.

So now we are inextricably woven. I have gathered together all the fragments. I return them to you. You have run with the wind, scattering and dissolving. I have run behind you, like your own shadow, gathering what you have sown in deep coffers.

I AM THE OTHER FACE OF YOU

Our faces are soldered together by soft hair, soldered together, showing two profiles of the same soul. Even when I passed through a room like a breath, I made others uneasy and they knew I had passed.

I was the white flame of your breath, your simoun breath shrivelling the world. I borrowed your visibility and it was through you I made my imprint on the world. I praised my own flame in you.

THIS IS THE BOOK YOU WROTE

AND YOU ARE THE WOMAN

I AM

Only our faces must shine twofold —like day and night— always separated by space and the evolutions of time.

The smoke sent my head to the ceiling: there it hung, looking down upon frog eyes, straw hair, mouth of soiled leather, mirrors of bald heads, furred monkey hands with ham colored palms. The music whipped the past out of its tomb and mummies flagellated my memory.

If Sabina were now a memory; if I should sit here and she should never come again! If I only imagined her one night because the drug made fine incisions and arranged the layers of my body on Persian silk hammocks, tipped with cotton each fine nerve and sent the radium arrows of fantasy through the flesh . . .

I am freezing and my head falls down through a thin film of smoke. I am searching for Sabina again with deep anguish through the faceless crowd.

I am ill with the obstinacy of images, reflections in cracked mirrors. I am a woman with Siamese cat eyes smiling always behind my gravest words, mocking my own intensity. I smile because I listen to the OTHER and I believe the OTHER. I am a marionette pulled by unskilled fingers, pulled apart, inharmoniously dislocated; one arm dead, the other rhapsodizing in mid-air. I laugh, not when it fits into my talk, but when it fits into the undercurrents of my talk. I want to know what is running underneath thus punctuated by bitter upheavals. The two currents do not meet. I see two women in me freakishly bound together, like circus twins. I see them tearing away from each other. I can hear the tearing, the anger and love, passion and pity. When the act of dislocation suddenly ceases —or when I cease to be aware of the sound— then the silence is more terrible because there is nothing but insanity around me, the insanity of things pulling, pulling within oneself, the roots tearing at each other to grow separately, the strain made to achieve unity.

It requires only a bar of music to still the dislocation for a moment; but there comes the smile again, and I know that the two of us have leaped beyond cohesion.

Greyness is no ordinary greyness, but a vast lead roof which covers the world like the lid of a soup pan. The breath of human beings is like the steam of a laundry house. The smoke of cigarettes is like a rain of ashes from Vesuvius. The lights taste of sulphur, and each face stares at you with the immensity of its defects. The smallness of a room is like that of an iron cage in which one can neither sit nor lie down. The largeness of other rooms is like a mortal danger always suspended above you, awaiting the moment of your joy to fall. Laughter and tears are not separate experiences, with intervals of rest: they rush out together and it is like walking with a sword between your legs. Rain does not wet your hair but drips in the cells of the brain with the obstinacy of a leak. Snow does not freeze the hands, but like ether distends the lungs until they burst. All the ships are sinking with fire in their bowels, and there are fires hissing in the cellars of every house. The loved one's whitest flesh is what the broken glass will cut and the wheel crush. The long howls in the night are howls of death. Night is the collaborator of torturers. Day is the light on harrowing discoveries. If a dog barks it is the man who loves wide gashes leaping in through the window. Laughter precedes hysteria. I am waiting for the heavy fall and the foam at the mouth.

A room with a ceiling threatening me like a pair of open scissors. Attic windows. I lie on a bed like gravel. All connections are breaking. Slowly I part from each being I love, slowly, carefully, completely. I tell them what I owe them and what they owe me. I cull their last glances and the last orgasm. My house is empty, sunglazed, reflectively alive, its stillness gathering implications, secret images which some day will madden me when I stand before blank walls, hearing far too much and seeing more than is humanly bearable. I part from them all. I die in a small scissor-arched room, dispossessed of my loves and my belongings, not even registered in the hotel book. At the same time I know that if I stayed in this room a few days an entirely new life could begin—like the soldering of human flesh after an operation. It is the terror of this new life, more than the terror of dying, which arouses me. I jump out of bed and run out of this room growing around me like a poisoned web, seizing my imagination, gnawing into my memory so that in seven moments I will forget who I am and whom I have loved.

It was room number 35 in which I might have awakened next morning mad or a whore.

Desire which had stretched the nerve broke, and each nerve seemed to break separately, continuously, making incisions, and acid ran instead of blood. I writhed within my own life, seeking a free avenue to carry the molten cries, to melt the pain into a cauldron of words for everyone to dip into, everyone who sought words for their own pain. What an enormous cauldron I stir now; enormous mouthfuls of acid I feed the others now, words bitter enough to burn all bitterness.

Disrupt the brown crust of the earth and all the sea will rise; the sea-anemones will float over my bed, and the dead ships will end their voyages in my garden. Exorcise the demons who ring the hours over my head at night when all counting should be suspended; they ring because they know that in my dreams I am cheating them of centuries. It must be counted like an hour against me.

I heard the lutes which were brought from Arabia and felt in my breasts the currents of liquid fire which run through the rooms of the Alhambra and refresh me from the too clear waters.

The too clear pain of love divided, love divided . . .

I was in a ship of sapphire sailing on seas of coral. And standing at the prow singing. My singing swelled the sails and ripped them; where they had been ripped the edge was burnt and the clouds too were ripped to tatters by my voice.

I saw a city where each house stood on a rock between black seas full of purple serpents hissing alarms, licking the rocks and peering over the walls of their garden with bulbous eyes.

I saw the glass palm tree sway before my eyes; the palm trees on my island were still and dusty when I saw them deadened by pain. Green leaves withered for me, and all the trees seemed glassily unresponsive while the glass palm tree threw off a new leaf on the very tip and climax of its head.

The white path sprouted from the heart of the white house and was edged with bristly cactus long-fingered and furry, unmoved by the wind, ageless. Over the ageless cactus the bamboo shoots trembled, close together, perpetually wind-shirred.

The house had the shape of an egg, and it was carpeted with cotton and windowless; one slept in the down and heard through the shell the street organ and the apple vendor who could not find the bell.

Images—bringing a dissolution of the soul within the body like the rupture of sweet-acid of the orgasm. Images made the blood run back and forth, and the watchfulness of the mind watching against dangerous ecstasies was now useless. Reality was drowned and fantasies choked each hour of the day.

Nothing seems true today except the death of the goldfish who used to make love at ninety kilometers an hour in the pool. The maid has given him a Christian burial. To the worms! To the worms!

AM floating again. All the facts and all the words, all images, all presages are sweeping over me, mocking each other. The dream! The dream! The dream rings through me like a giant copper bell when I wish to betray it. It brushes by me with bat wings when I open human eyes and seek to live dreamlessly. When human pain has struck me fiercely, when anger has corroded me, I rise, I always rise after the crucifixion, and I am in terror of my ascensions. THE FISSURE IN REALITY. The divine departure. I fall. I fall into darkness after the collision with pain, and after pain the divine departure.

Oh, the weight, the tremendous weight of my head pulled up by the clouds and swinging in space, the body like a wisp of straw, the clouds dragging my hair like a scarf caught in a chariot wheel, the body dangling, colliding with the lantern stars, the clouds dragging me over the world.

I cannot stop, or descend.

I hear the unfurling of water, of skies and curtains. I hear the shiver of leaves, the breathing of the air, the wailing of the unborn, the pressure of the wind.

I hear the movements of the stars and planets, the slight rust creak when they shift their position. The silken passage of radiations, the breath of circles turning.

I hear the passing of mysteries and the breathing of monsters. Overtones only, or undertones. Collision with reality blurs my vision and submerges me into the dream. I feel the distance like a wound. It unrolls itself before me like the rug before the steps of a cathedral for a wedding or a burial. It is unrolled like a crimson bride between the others and me, but I cannot walk on it without a feeling of uneasiness, as one has at ceremonies. The ceremony of walking along the unrolled carpet into the cathedral where the functions unravel to which I am a stranger. I neither marry nor die. And the distance between the crowd, between the others and me, grows wider.

Distance. I never walked over the carpet into the ceremonies. Into the fullness of the crowd life, into the authentic music and the odor of men. I never attended the wedding or the burial. Everything for me took place either in the belfry where I was alone with the deafening sound of bells calling in iron voices, or in the cellar where I nibbled at the candles and the incense stored away with the mice.

I cannot be certain of any event or place, only of my solitude. Tell me what the stars are saying about me. Does Saturn have eyes made of onions which weep all the time? Has Mercury chicken feathers on his heels, and does Mars wear a gas mask? Gemini, the evolved twins, do they evolve all the time, turning on a spit, Gemini a la broche?

There is a fissure in my vision and madness will always rush through. Lean over me, at the bedside of my madness, and let me stand without crutches.

I am an insane woman for whom houses wink and open their bellies. Significance stares at me from everywhere, like a gigantic underlying ghostliness. Significance emerges out of dank alleys and sombre faces, leans out of the windows of strange houses. I am constantly reconstructing a pattern of something forever lost and which I cannot forget. I catch the odors of the past on street corners and I am aware of the men who will be born tomorrow. Behind windows there are either enemies or worshippers. Never neutrality or passivity. Always intention and premeditation. Even stones have for me druidical expressions.

I walk ahead of myself in perpetual expectancy of miracles.

I am enmeshed in my lies, and I want absolution. I cannot tell the truth because I have felt the heads of men in my womb. The truth would be death-dealing and I prefer fairytales. I am wrapped in lies which do not penetrate my soul. As if the lies I tell were like costumes. The shell of mystery can break and grow again over night. But the moment I step into the cavern of my lies I drop into darkness. I see a face which stares at me like the glance of a cross-eyed man.

I remember the cold on Jupiter freezing ammonia and out of ammonia crystals came the angels. Bands of ammonia and methane encircling Uranus. I remember the tornadoes of inflammable methane on Saturn. I remember on Mars a vegetation like the tussock grasses of Peru and Patagonia, an ochrous red, a rusty ore vegetation, mosses and lichens. Iron bearing red clays and red sandstone. Light there had a sound and sunlight was an orchestra.

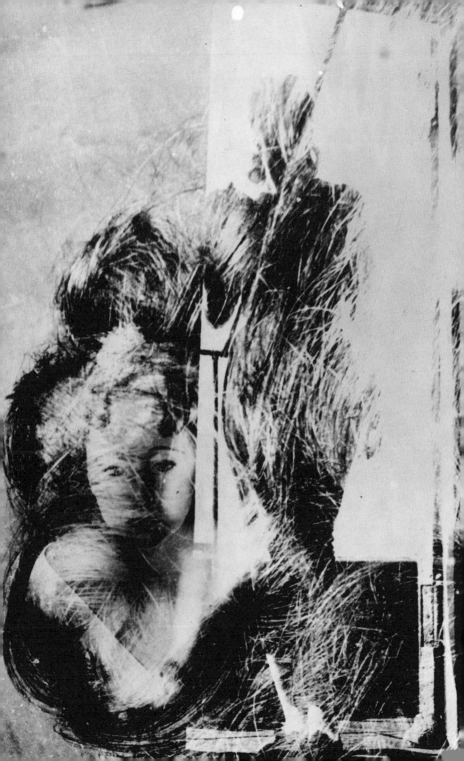

DILATED eyes, noble-raced profile, wilful mouth. Jeanne, all in fur, with fur eyelashes, walking with head carried high, nose to the wind, eyes on the stars, walking imperiously, dragging her crippled leg. Her eyes higher than the human level, her leg limping behind the tall body, inert, like the chained ball of a prisoner.

Prisoner on earth, against her will to die.

Her leg dragging so that she might remain on earth, a heavy dead leg which she carried like the ball and chain of a prisoner.

Her pale, nerve-stained fingers tortured the guitar, tormenting and twisting the strings with her timidity as her low voice sang; and behind her song, her thirst, her hunger and her fears. As she turned the keys of her guitar, fiercely tuning

43

it, the string snapped and her eyes were terror-striken as by the snapping of her universe.

She sang and she laughed: I love my brother.

I love my brother. I want crusades and martyrdom. I find the world too small.

Salted tears of defeat crystallized in the corners of her restless eyes.

But I never weep.

She picked up a mirror and looked at herself with love.

Narcisse gazing at himself in Lanvin mirrors. The Four Horsemen of the Apocalypse riding through the Bois. Tragedy rolling on cord tires.

The world is too small. I get tired of playing the guitar, of knitting, and walking, and bearing children. Men are small, and passions are short-lived. I get furious at stairways, furious at doors, at walls, furious at everyday life which interferes with the continuity of ecstasy.

But there is a martyrdom of tenseness, of fever, of living continuously like the firmament in full movement and in full effulgence.

You never saw the stars grow weary or dim. They never sleep.

She sat looking at herself in a hand mirror and

searching for an eyelash which had fallen into her eye.

I married a man, Jeanne said, who had never seen painted eyes weep, and on the day of my wedding I wept. He looked at me and he saw a woman shedding enormous black tears, very black tears. It frightened him to see me shedding black tears on my wedding night. When I heard the bells ringing I thought they rang far too loud. They deafened me. I felt I would begin to weep blood, my ears hurt me so much. I coughed because the din was immense and terrifying, like the time I stood next to the bells of Chartres. He said the bells were not loud at all, but I heard them so close to me that I could not hear his voice, and the noise seemed like hammering against my flesh, and I thought my ears would burst. Every cell in my body began to burst, one by one, inside of the immense din from which I could not escape. I tried to run away from the bells. I shouted: stop the bells from ringing! But I could not run away from them because the sound was all round me and inside me, like my heart pounding in huge iron beats, like my arteries clamping like cymbals, like my head knocked against granite and a hammer striking the vein on my temple. Explosions of sounds without respite which made my cells burst, and the echoes of the cracking and breaking in me rolled into echoes, struck me again and again until my nerves were twisting and curling inside me, and then snapped and tore at the gong, until my flesh contracted and shrivelled with pain, and the blood spilled out of my ears and I could not bear any more . . . Could not bear to attend my own wedding, could not bear to be married to man, because, because, because . . .

I LOVE MY BROTHER!

She shook her heavy Indian bracelets; she caressed her Orient blue bottles, and then she lay down again.

I am the most tired woman in the world. I am tired when I get up. Life requires an effort which I cannot make. Please give me that heavy book. I need to put something heavy like that on top of my head. I have to place my feet under the pillows always, so as to be able to stay on earth. Otherwise I feel myself going away, going away at a tremendous speed, on account of my lightness. I know that I am dead. As soon as I utter a phrase my sincerity dies, becomes a lie whose coldness chills me. Don't say anything, because I see that you understand me, and I am afraid of your understanding. I have such a fear of finding another like myself, and such a desire to find one! I am so utterly lonely, but I also have such a fear that my isolation be broken through, and I no longer be the head and ruler of my universe. I am in great terror of your understanding by which you penetrate into my world; and then I stand revealed and I have to share my kingdom with you.

But Jeanne, fear of madness, only the fear of madness will drive us out of the precincts of our solitude, out of the sacredness of our solitude. The fear of madness will burn down the walls of our secret house and send us out into the world seeking warm contact. Worlds self-made and self-nourished are so full of ghosts and monsters.

Knowing only fear, it is true, such a fear that it chokes me, that I stand gaping and breathless, like a person deprived of air; or at other times, I cannot hear, I suddenly become deaf to the world. I stamp my feet and hear nothing. I shout and hear nothing of my shout. And then at times, when I lie in bed, fear clutches me again, a great terror of silence and of what will come out of this silence towards me and knock on the walls of my temples, a great mounting, choking fear. I knock on the wall, on the floor, to drive the silence away. I knock and I sing and I whistle persistently until I drive the fear away.

When I sit before my mirror I laugh at myself. I am brushing my hair. Here are a pair of eyes, two long braids, two feet. I look at them like dice in a box, wondering if I should shake them, would they still come out and be ME. I cannot tell how all these separate pieces can be ME. I do not exist. I am not a body. When I shake hands I feel that the person is so far away that he is in the other room, and that my hand is in the other room. When I blow my nose I have a fear that it might remain on the handkerchief.

Voice like a mistlethrush. The shadow of death running after each word so that they wither before she has finished uttering them.

When my brother sat in the sun and his face was shadowed on the back of the chair I kissed his shadow. I kissed his shadow and this kiss did not touch him, this kiss was lost in the air and melted with the shadow. Our love of each other is like one long shadow kissing, without hope of reality.

SHE led me into the house of incest. It was the only house which was not included in the twelve houses of the zodiac. It could neither be reached by the route of the milky way, nor by the glass ship through whose transparent bottom one could follow the outline of the lost continents, nor by following the arrows pointing the direction of the wind, nor by following the voice of the mountain echoes.

The rooms were chained together by steps— no room was on a level with another— and all the steps were deeply worn. There were windows between the rooms, little spying-eyed windows, so that one might talk in the dark from room to room, without seeing the other's face. The rooms were filled with the rhythmic heaving of the sea coming from many sea-shells. The windows gave out on a static sea, where immobile fishes had been glued to painted backgrounds. Everything had been made to stand still in the house of incest, because they all had such a fear of movement and warmth, such a fear that all love and all life should flow out of reach and be lost!

Everything had been made to stand still, and everything was rotting away. The sun had been nailed in the roof of the sky and the moon beaten deep into its Oriental niche.

In the house of incest there was a room which could not be found, a room without window, the fortress of their love, a room without window where the mind and blood coalesced in a union without orgasm and rootless like those of fishes. The promiscuity of glances, of phrases, like sparks marrying in space. The collision between their resemblances, shedding the odor of tamarisk and sand, of rotted shells and dying sea-weeds, their love like the ink of squids, a banquet of poisons.

Stumbling from room to room I came into the room of paintings, and there sat Lot with his hand upon his daughter's breast while the city burned behind them, cracking open and falling into the sea. There where he sat with his daughter the Oriental rug was red and stiff, but the turmoil which shook them showed through the rocks splitting around them, through the earth yawning beneath their feet, through the trees flaming

up like torches, through the sky smoking and smouldering red, all cracking with the joy and terror of their love. Joy of the father's hand upon the daughter's breast, the joy of the fear racking her. Her costume tightly pressed around her so that her breasts heave and swell under his fingers, while the city is rent by lightning, and spits under the teeth of fire, great blocks of a gaping ripped city sinking with the horror of obscenity, and falling into the sea with the hiss of the eternally damned. No cry of horror from Lot and his daughter but from the city in flames, from an un-quenchable desire of father and daughter, of brother and sister, mother and son.

I looked upon a clock to find the truth. The hours were passing like ivory chess figures, strik-ing piano notes, and the minutes raced on wires mounted like tin soldiers. Hours like tall ebony women with gongs between their legs, tolling continuously so that I could not count them. I heard the tolling of my heart-beats; I heard the footsteps of my dreams, and the beat of time was lost among them like the face of truth.

I came upon a forest of decapitated trees, women carved out of bamboo, flesh slatted like that of slaves in joyless slavery, faces cut in two by the sculptor's knife, showing two sides for-ever separate, eternally two-faced, and it was I who had to shift about to behold the entire woman. Truncated undecagon figures, eleven sides, eleven angles, in veined and vulnerable woods, fragments of bodies, bodies armless and headless. The torso of a tube-rose, the knee of Achilles, tubercles and excrescences, the foot of a mummy in rotted wood, the veined docile wood carved into human contortions. The forest must weep and bend like the shoulders of men, dead figures inside of live trees. A forest animated now with intellectual faces, intellectual contortions. Trees become man and woman, two-faced, nostalgic for the shivering of leaves. Trees reclining, woods shining, and the forest trembling with rebellion so bitter I heard its wailing within its deep forest consciousness. Wailing the loss of its leaves and the failure of transmutation.

Further a forest of white plaster, white plaster eggs. Large white eggs on silver disks, an elegy to birth, each egg a promise, each half-shaped nascence of man or woman or animal not yet precise. Womb and seed and egg, the moist beginning being worshipped rather than its flowering. The eggs so white, so still, gave birth to hope without breaking, but the cut-down tree lying there produced a green live branch that laughed at the sculptor.

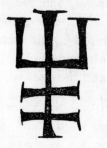

JEANNE opened all the doors and searched through all the rooms. In each room the startled guest blinked with surprise. She asked them: "Please hang up something out of your windows. Hang up a shawl, or a colored handkerchief, or a rug. I am going out into the garden. I want to see how many windows can be accounted for. I may thus find the room where my brother is hiding from me. I have lost my brother. I beg you, help me, every one of you." She pulled shawls off the tables, she took a red curtain down, a coral bedspread, a Chinese panel, and hung them out of the windows herself.

Then she rushed out into the garden of dead trees, over the lava paths, over the micha schist, and all the minerals on her path burned, the muscovite like a bride, the pyrite, the hydrous silica, the cinnabar, the azurite like a fragment of benefic Jupiter, the malachite, all crushed together, pressed together, melted jewels, melted planets, alchemized by air and sun and time and space, mixed into mineral fixity, the fixity of the fear of death and the fear of life.

Semen dried into the silence of rock and mineral. The words we did not shout, the tears unshed, the curse we swallowed, the phrase we shortened, the love we killed, turned into magnetic iron ore, into tourmaline, into pyrate agate, blood congealed into cinnabar, blood calcinated, leadened into galena, oxidized, aluminized, sulphated, calcinated, the mineral glow of dead meteors and exhausted suns in the forest of dead trees and dead desires.

Standing on a hill of orthoclase, with topaz and argentite stains on her hands, she looked up at the facade of the house of incest, the rusty ore facade of the house of incest, and there was one window with the blind shut tight and rusty, one window without light like a dead eye, choked by the hairy long arm of old ivy.

She trembled with the desire not to shriek, an effort so immense that she stood still, her blood unseen for the golden pallor of her face.

She struggled with her death coming: I do not love anyone; I love no one, not even my brother. I love nothing but this absence of pain, this cold neutral absence of pain.

Standing still for many years, between the moment she had lost her brother and the moment she had looked at the facade of the house of incest, moving in endless circles round the corners of the dreams, never reaching the end of her voyage, she apprehended all wonder through the rock-agedness of her pain, by dying.

And she found her brother asleep among the paintings.

Jeanne, I fell asleep among the paintings, where I could sit for many days worshipping your portrait. I fell in love with your portrait, Jeanne, because it will never change. I have such a fear of seeing you grow old, Jeanne; I fell in love with an unchanging you that will never be taken away from me. I was wishing you would die, so that no one could take you away from me, and I would love the painting of you as you would look eternally.

They bowed to one part of themselves only— their likeness.

Good night, my brother!

Good night, Jeanne!

With her walked distended shadows, stigmatized by fear. They carried their compact like a jewel on their breast; they wore it proudly like their coat of arms.

WALKED into my own book, seeking peace. It was night, and I made a careless movement inside the dream; I turned too brusquely the corner and I bruised myself against my madness. It was this seeing too much, this seeing of a tragedy in the quiver of an eyelid, constructing a crime in the next room, the men and women who had loved before me on the same hotel bed.

I carry white sponges of knowledge on strings of nerves.

As I move within my book I am cut by pointed glass and broken bottles in which there is still the odor of sperm and perfume.

More pages added to the book but pages like a prisoner's walking back and forth over the space allotted him. What is it allotted me to say?

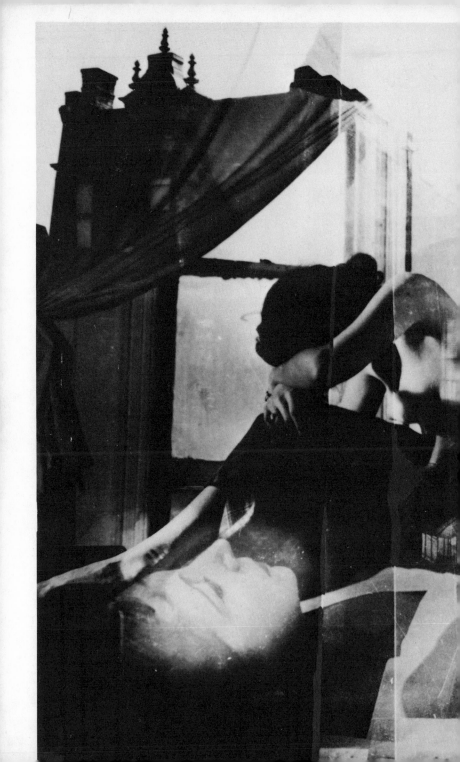

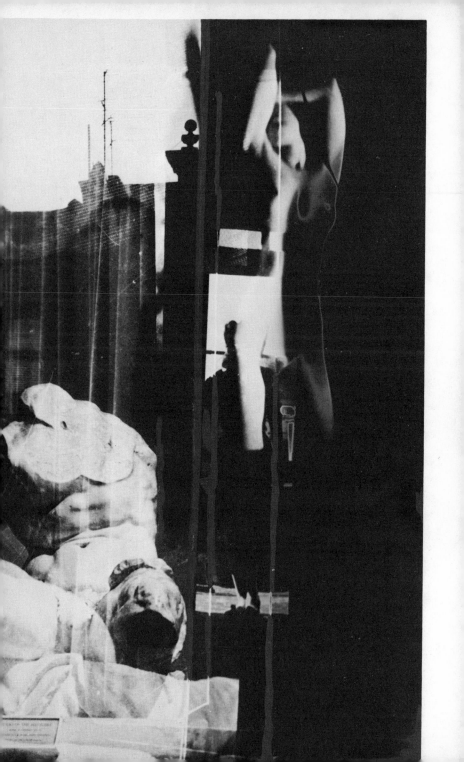

Only the truth disguised in a fairytale, and this is the fairytale behind which all the truths are staring as behind grilled mosque windows. With veils. The moment I step into the cavern of my lies I drop into darkness, and see a mask which stares at me like the glance of a cross-eyed man; yet I am wrapped in lies which do not penetrate my soul, as if the lies I tell were like costumes.

LIES CREATE SOLITUDE

I walked out of my book into the paralytic's room.

He sat there among many objects under glass as in a museum. He had collected a box of paint which he never painted with, a thousand books with pages uncut, and they were covered with dust. His Spanish cape hung on the shoulders of a mannequin, his guitar lay with strings snapped like long disordered hair. He sat before a note book of blank pages, saying: I swallow my own words. I chew and chew everything until it deteriorates. Every thought or impulse I have is chewed into nothingness. I want to capture all my thoughts at once, but they run in all directions. If I could do this I would be capturing the nimblest of minds, like a shoal of minnows. I would reveal innocence and duplicity, generosity and calculation, fear and cowardice and courage. I want to tell the whole truth, but I cannot tell the whole truth because I would have to write four pages at once, like four long columns simultaneously, four pages to the present one, and so I do not write at all. I would have to write backwards, retrace my steps constantly to catch the echoes and the overtones.

His skin was transparent like that of a newborn child, and his eyes green like moss. He bowed to Sabina, to Jeanne, and to me: meet the modern Christ, who is crucified by his own nerves, for all our neurotic sins!

The modern Christ was wiping the perspiration which dripped over his face, as if he were sitting there in the agony of a secret torture. Pain-carved features. Eyes too open, as if dilated by scenes of horror. Heavy-lidded, with a world-heavy fatigue. Sitting on his chair as if there were ghosts standing beside him. A smile like an insult. Lips edged and withered by the black scum of drugs. A body taut like wire.

In our writings we are brothers, I said. The speed of our vertigoes is the same. We arrived at the same place at the same moment, which is not so with other people's thoughts. The language of nerves which we both use makes us brothers in writing.

The modern Christ said: I was born without a

skin. I dreamed once that I stood naked in a garden and that it was carefully and neatly peeled, like a fruit. Not an inch of skin left on my body. It was all gently pulled off, all of it, and then I was told to walk, to live, to run. I walked slowly at first, and the garden was very soft, and I felt the softness of the garden so acutely, not on the surface of my body, but all through it, the soft warm air and the perfumes penetrated me like needles through every open bleeding pore. All the pores open and breathing the soft-ness, the warmth, and the smells. The whole body invaded, penetrated, responding, every tiny cell and pore active and breathing and trembling and enjoying. I shrieked with pain. I ran. And as I ran the wind lashed me, and then the voices of people like whips on me. Being touched! Do you know what it is to be touched by a human being!

He wiped his face with his handkerchief.

The paralytic sat still in the corner of the room.

You are fortunate, he said, you are fortunate to feel so much; I wish I could feel all that. You are at least alive to pain, whereas I . . .

Then he turned his face away, and just before he turned away I saw the veins on his forehead swelling, swelling with the effort he made, the inner effort which neither his tongue nor his body, nor his thoughts would obey.

If only we could all escape from this house of incest, where we only love ourselves in the other, if only I could save you all from yourselves, said the modern Christ.

But none of us could bear to pass through the tunnel which led from the house into the world on the other side of the walls, where there were leaves on the trees, where water ran beside the paths, where there was daylight and joy. We could not believe that the tunnel would open on daylight: we feared to be trapped into darkness again; we feared to return whence we had come, from darkness and night. The tunnel would narrow and taper down as we walked; it would close around us, and close tighter and tighter around us and stifle us. It would grow heavy and narrow and suffocate us as we walked.

Yet we knew that beyond the house of incest there was daylight, and none of us could walk towards it.

We all looked now at the dancer who stood at the center of the room dancing the dance of the woman without arms. She danced as if she were deaf and could not follow the rhythm of the music. She danced as if she could not hear the sound of her castanets. Her dancing was isolated and separated from music and from us and from the room and from life. The castanets sounded like the steps of a ghost.

She danced, laughing and sighing and breathing all for herself. She danced her fears, stopping in the center of every dance to listen to reproaches that we could not hear, or bowing to applause that we did not make. She was listening to a music we could not hear, moved by hallucinations we could not see.

My arms were taken away from me, she sang. I was punished for clinging. I clung. I clutched all those I loved; I clutched at the lovely moments of life; my hands closed upon every full hour. My arms were always tight and craving to embrace. I wanted to embrace and hold the light, the wind, the sun, the night, the whole world. I wanted to caress, to heal, to rock, to lull, to surround, to encompass. And I strained and I held so much that they broke; they broke away from me. Everything eluded me then. I was condemned not to hold.

Trembling and shaking she stood looking at her arms now stretched before her again.

She looked at her hands tightly closed and opened them slowly, opened them completely like Christ; she opened them in a gesture of abandon and giving; she relinquished and forgave, opening her arms and her hands, permitting all things to flow away and beyond her.

I could not bear the passing of things. All flowing, all passing, all movement choked me with anguish.

And she danced; she danced with the music and with the rhythm of earth's circles; she turned with the earth turning, like a disk, turning all faces to light and to darkness evenly, dancing towards daylight.